Starting

Story by W
Pictures by Ruth Benton

A LITTLE LION
Oxford · Batavia · Sydney

John was not very happy. He
was starting school.
  "I don't want to go to school,"
he said. "I like being at home."

"You're too old to stay home," said Mom. "You have to go to school."

"Home is fine with me," said John. "You stay home and you're older than I am."

"I don't want to go to school," said John. "I don't want to leave my friends, Joe and Emma and Wayne and Mario."

"You'll make lots of new friends," said Mom. "And Joe and Emma are going to school too."

"I like Wayne and Mario better," said John.

"I don't want to go to school," said John. "I'm scared of the teacher."

"You liked her when we met
her at the bookstore last week,"
said Mom.

"That was last week," said John.

"I don't want to go to school," said John. "It's too far away."

"It's not very far," said Mom.
"And there's a park next door.
You can play on the swings after
school."
"I shall be too tired. After all
that walking," said John.

"I don't want to go to school," said John. "You have to eat in the cafeteria."

"You can take sandwiches if you don't like cafeteria food," said Mom.

"I don't like sandwiches either," said John.

The Saturday before John
started school Mom took him into
town. She bought a pencil, a ruler
and a packet of felt-tip pens.

"I like felt-tip pens," said John.

"Good," said Mom. "They're
for school."

At the shoe store Mom asked
the man for some gym shoes.
   "Going to do some climbing
are you, lucky fellow," winked
the man. "All those ropes and
trampolines in the school gym.
Wish I was young again."
   "We haven't got a gym," said John.
   "They have at school," said Mom.

In the toy store Mom looked at the lunch boxes while John looked at the Lego blocks.

"Would you like a red box, or a blue one?" Mom asked.

"I'd rather have some Lego blocks," said John.

"You'd look pretty silly carrying your lunch to school in a box made out of Lego blocks," said Mom. "I don't think it would last very long."

As they came out of the store
they met Jason. Jason was older
than John. He already went to
school.

"You'll like it at school," he said.

"You can play softball on the grass
at recess. Who's your teacher?"
  John told him.
  "Lucky you," said Jason.
"Everybody likes her."

On Monday morning Mom put John's gym shoes, pencil, ruler and felt-tips in his school bag. She packed the lunch box with potato chips, carrot sticks, a hard-boiled egg, an apple, and a thermos of milk.

"See, no sandwiches," she said. "Are you still worried about going to school?"

"Just a bit," said John. "I wish
you could stay with me."

"I don't expect I can," said Mom. "If all the moms stayed there would be no room in the classroom for the children. I know someone who will be there though."

"Jason," said John.

"No. Jason's in another class. Look. Here's something else for you to put in your bag."

Mom handed him a bookmark with a red tassle. "I am with you always," she read.

"That's Jesus, isn't it?" said John.

"Yes," said Mom.

"Do you think he likes softball?" said John. "Jason says we can play softball at recess. I wouldn't want to leave him on the sidelines."

"I don't think Jesus will ever stay on the sidelines," said Mom.

"Good," said John, picking up his bag and lunch box. "Are you ready? I don't want to be late the first day."

Copyright © 1989 Wendy Green
Illustrations copyright © 1989 Lion Publishing

Published by
Lion Publishing Corporation
1705 Hubbard Avenue, Batavia, Illinois 60510, USA
ISBN 0 7459 1739 9

First published 1989

Printed and bound in Yugoslavia